THE ARRANGEMENT

Vol. 13

H.M. Ward

www.SexyAwesomeBooks.com

H.M. Ward Press

COPYRIGHT

This book is a work of fiction. Names, characters, places, and incidents are either the product of the author's imagination or are used fictitiously, and any resemblance to actual persons, living or dead, events, or locales is entirely coincidental.

H.M. WARD PRESS
First Edition: Jan 2014
ISBN: 978-1-63035-016-1

THE ARRANGEMENT

Vol. 13

CHAPTER 1

~SEAN~

No matter what the glint means, it's bad. My mind races through semi-coherent thoughts—images—of what Avery saw, but my mind is sluggish and lust ridden. She's finally coming out of her shell, finally denying that mundane version of her sexual being. I have her naked body pressed firmly to the cold window. I can only imagine how hot she must look from the other side of the pane, but the fact that she even does it astounds me. I put her on display as if I own every inch of her, and she lets me. It's almost as if she likes it, and I hope to God that she does.

The way her body fits against mine is perfect. I slip my palm over the swell of her hips and cup her breasts while kissing the side of her neck. There's a spot that makes her weak. When I find it, she gives in and does anything and everything. Sometimes I think she's guarding that area, trying to keep me away. Other times, like now, I think she wants me there, kissing her senseless and doing anything I need.

Avery breathes in and pushes back against me, so I pin her harder. She gasps. The small sound always pulls my lips into a smile. I manage to undo my jeans and press my hard length to her back. That sound purrs from deep within her again. God, I love it when she does that. That little breath sounds like ecstasy, shock, and desire all wrapped into one tiny perfect noise.

I grab her hips, angling them so I can take her. I planned on waiting and teasing her more, but I can't. Not when she's like this. Avery presses back into me and tells me how much she wants me inside of her.

Her words undo me.

Pressing my hands firmly to the sides of her hips, I move until we line up perfectly and push into her. Avery gasps again and claws at the window. Arching her back, she presses her hips toward me, taking my cock in deeper.

She's so fucking wet that I can't think beyond the moment, which is rare. I'm always ten steps ahead of everyone. It's part of who I am, but here—in this second—I'm lost. A lifetime of pain vanishes with every thrust into her hot, slick core. The past vanishes and I feel alive.

I tangle our fingers together and don't want to stop. Pushing harder and deeper with every thrust, Avery takes me and begs for more. I didn't think I'd have this chance.

For years I've walked around feeling nothing, to the point that I'd become a monster. I'm not some dipshit who can't admit what he is—what he's become. I know damn well that I'm a lost cause, that there's nothing left to save, and yet, this woman brings me back to life. I was a corpse, and completely apathetic, and now my heart is racing and my body is covered in sweat, shaking, because I can't get enough of her.

I want more, she always makes me want more, and it's not just her body—it's her—it's Avery. There's something about the quirky smile on her sinful lips and the way she speaks. It's the flash of her eyes when she sees something commonplace and finds joy in it. The woman is bursting with life, even though when I met her, I wasn't sure she wanted to be.

The darkness within her called to me. It's been my destruction and my savior, because it brought me to this woman and kept me coming back for more.

Every inch of my body is tense and I can't stand it anymore. I need to hear her lose it, and call out my name. Dropping my hands to her hips, I pummel into her harder and faster until she melts into me. At least that's my plan.

I want Avery to forget all the shit that's bothering her, I want those nightmares to abate for just one night, and I want to be the reason.

I hope to God she needs me as much as I need her. Avery's become my air, sunlight, and darkness—everything I need. Life without her would be unimaginable.

That's when Avery mentions the light—the glint in the darkness. Before I have a chance to sate her, I pull us to the floor. I'm not sure if paparazzi found us or if it's something worse because I didn't see it. Either way, I'm not chancing it.

A second later, there's a loud cracking noise, followed by the window blowing to bits. Glass fragments blast past us. I try to cover Avery, but I can't look up to see how much of her skin is exposed. My jeans save my legs from the shards, but not my arms and back. A searing, hot pain shoots through my shoulder and down my arm.

Avery shakes beneath me, as her nails bite into my shoulders. I know she's trying to wrap her arms around me, but I pin her to the floor, not allowing her to move.

The moment lasts forever, giving enough time for ancient worries to reseed themselves in my mind. They spring up like weeds and vine faster than I can uproot them and toss them into the fire.

That dreadful thought whispers in my mind, *What if you can't protect her? What if she dies?*

That's what does it. No matter how hard I fight it, I'm pulled into the past, into that goddamn memory that I try so hard to forget. Images flash through my mind like a slideshow: Amanda's limp hand and curled fingers, pale and cold with dark blood pooled under her snow-white skin. I stand there seeing myself from above as if trapped in a nightmare.

Then I'm there, sucked into the past, standing in the doorway to our old room, and the emotions come surging back. The insides of my body feel like they're being crushed. Amanda called me and begged for help, but I didn't come.

This is my fault.

CHAPTER 2

~SEAN~

I stand there shaking from guilt, rage, and grief. I know my wife is gone, but I refuse to accept it. I race to her side and pick up her cold, stiff hand, and that's when I notice the baby covered in blood, lifeless and silent. My daughter is so tiny and the way she lies silently by Amanda, with those tiny fingers and toes, kills me.

Jaw trembling, my throat tightens and I try to force the anguish back, but it's consuming me. Piece by piece, I feel my mind slip away.

That moment destroyed me and it was my fault.

When I blink, I feel Avery beneath my body, but the ghosts won't release me. I choke and realize the room is silent—like before. Images from that night long ago continue to bombard me, flashing in and out of my mind, clouding the present with the past. I can't stop it.

"Avery?" I ask her, shaking her slightly because she's so still. "Are you all right?" My voice is far from steady, and as I pull back to look at her, I see that she's lying in a pool of scarlet. A shiver takes hold of my soul and won't release me. Incoherently, I stutter something else, but she doesn't speak.

My mind fractures. I feel it coming apart as if it were a puzzle lifted from a table. One by one, rationality falls away. I want to go after whoever did this to us, but I can't leave Avery. I call her name over and over again, before lifting her still body from the glass.

Pieces of the window glitter like diamonds on the floor. I walk her over to the far side of the house, out of sight of the window, and lay her on the couch. Her dark lashes flutter and she looks up at me with those eyes. "Sean?" her voice is scratchy, like she's going to cry. Her arm has a long gash and is bleeding. She reaches for it and pulls her hand away.

Avery examines her bright red fingers and then looks up at me. Ignoring her own injury, she asks, "Are you hurt?" I can't speak. There's no way to answer that question and confess what this did to me. I don't want to lie, so I say nothing.

Working quickly, I grab my shirt and bandage her arm. I don't see any glass lodged under the skin, but that doesn't mean it's not there. Images of Amanda flicker behind my eyes and mix with the present until I don't know which reality is genuine.

I caused this. The thought races through my mind, replaying over and over again.

Breathe, Sean. Hold it together. I say these things inside my head, but can't manage to find words for Avery. She lets me wrap up her wound and look her over quickly. When

I decide she isn't going to hemorrhage, everything snaps back to the present and my attention shifts to the fucker who did this.

"Stay." It's the only word I can manage. Turning quickly, I race across the room and find the spot in the corner, where the stairs would have been. I pull the molding free and yank out the gun that brought me so much misery, and load it. I grab my jacket and pull it on before walking over to her.

Avery watches in silence with her beautiful face full of fear. "Don't do it. Don't go." She clutches at my collar which makes ribbons of scarlet flow down her arm from beneath the makeshift bandage.

I hate the fear in her voice, but I can't let this fucker walk away. I say things, I don't even know what, but I kiss her cheek, shove the gun into her hands, and a horrible premonition claws at my heart. That gun took my wife and daughter from me. That gun destroyed me. Handing it to her feels wrong, but she needs it.

Wiping the sweat from my brow, I manage to keep my voice devoid of emotion. "Stay out of sight and if someone comes in, shoot them."

CHAPTER 3

~AVERY~

I'm trembling as Sean shoves the cold metal into my hand. When I look down, I see an old gun and instantly know what I'm holding—it's the weapon that took Amanda Ferro's life. My throat tightens, making his name come out like a squawk, "Sean, wait!"

But he doesn't stop. Unarmed, Sean strides across the room, zips his coat, and jumps out the shattered window to the ground far below. Horrified, I stand up and watch him disappear into the darkness. Fear courses through me and I think about going after him, but I've lost too much blood. The gash in my arm is dripping down my side and if I don't stay still, I'll pass out. As it is, the wound is throbbing, but the gun in my hand distracts me more.

I can't imagine what's going through Sean's mind. When those blue eyes locks with mine, something inside me cowers. They're cold, detached, and completely ruthless. Whoever did this is dead. I saw it on Sean's face, and I wonder. The act of handing me this gun had to suck him into his past in a very real way. Add in the blood and someone trying to shoot me...

As I think, I manage to pull on a pair of Sean's sweats, and that's when reality hits me. This wasn't an accident. Someone tried to kill me. I'd be dead right now if Sean hadn't pulled me to the floor. My knees give out and I sit down hard, clutching the gun against my chest like it's a teddy bear. Tears fill my eyes as terror overflows from my heart and trickles down my cheeks. I glance at the gun and can't stand to hold it. Leaning over, I place it on the floor and push it away with my foot, before sinking back into the couch. I grab a remote control and shut off all the lights. The darkness swallows me whole, and the only sounds I can hear are my pounding heart and the wind rustling the branches outside.

The room grows colder from the open window. I remain where I am, lost in shadows, on the couch, gripping my arm and holding it up to slow the bleeding. I'm not thinking about the wound or if I need stitches—I'm wondering about Sean.

As far as I could tell, he jumped out the window, defenseless. Whoever took the shot is long gone, at least I hope he is. I pull my knees into my chest, wishing I could vanish. I can't calm down and it feels like my chest is going to explode. It's as if I've been sitting here forever, and every little sound makes me jump as I watch through the window for signs of Sean.

That's when I hear it. The sound is barely there, but it makes my eyes grow wide and my pulse quicken. My head snaps toward the noise. I frantically look for Sean through the shattered window, but he's not there. I can't see anyone, but I hear footfalls inching closer, crunching their way through the dried grass and fallen leaves. The sound is softer than my breaths but it sounds like drums pounding in my ears.

The paces are too slow, too careful. My eyes dart through the night, seeking any sign of who's approaching. The person passes the window, out of sight, and is approaching the front door.

Sean's words ring in my ears over and over again, *If anyone comes in shoot them.*

I can't shoot someone. Killing a person, ending their life, even if they tried to kill me first—I can't do it. I glance at the gun on the floor and know it should be in my hand, but I can't touch it. That thing destroyed Sean's life. It feels like a bad omen to even look at it.

There's a scraping sound at the front door, a metal key sliding into the lock. The knob twists, and just before the door opens, I jump up and frantically look for a place to hide. There isn't anywhere obvious, so I act on instinct and dart across to the kitchen, tug open one of those huge cabinet doors, and duck inside. Crouching down as low as possible, I curl into a ball. My hands are around my ankles and I'm shivering all over.

A small slit is in front of me where the cabinet doors meet. It's not enough to see anything, but I know the person isn't Sean. If it was, he would have flipped on the lights and called out to me. This person is quiet, slowly walking across the floor. My heart slaps into my ribs so hard that I think they're going to crack. Biting my lips, I remain crouched, peering into the opening.

The man passes me, craning his neck from side to side, searching. Does he know his shot missed? Is he here to finish the job?

Dark boots pass the couch and then the bed. He stands to the side of the window and looks down at the blood on the floor. The way the moonlight catches the glass looks beautiful in a haunting way. Some of the shards glisten red, nearly black.

A scream is building inside of me and it's everything I can do to not release it. Where is Sean? My jaw is locked, biting hard to keep quiet.

When the man turns, I see a weapon in his hand—a rifle. He raises it and turns slowly, as if he heard my thoughts. He inches toward the bed and aims at the center of the mattress. He holds the gun there for half a beat and fires.

The sound does exactly what he wants—the blaring noise makes me jump and let out a small shriek. It slipped between my lips before I could stop it. The man turns in my direction. He knows where I am. I swear that he can see my eyes, because our gazes lock as he walks toward my hiding place.

My heart thumps harder as I begin to shake uncontrollably. I'm going to die. He's coming to kill me and I'm hiding in here like a coward. After everything I lived through, after everything I fought for, to be here now and have Sean's ring on my finger, after losing my parents, and becoming a fucking prostitute—this is how I die—hiding in a cabinet.

My fear rapidly shifts to anger. It isn't fair. Life isn't fair. As soon as something good happens to me, it's chased by death. Fuck that. I reach around to see what's near me and grab a bag. I rip it open, knowing that the crazy gunman already knows my location, and then reach blindly on the shelf with my other hand for something— anything.

Just as my hand lands on something useful, the man speaks, "Got ya."

He pulls the door open and I jump out at him like a deranged jack-in-the-box jerking the open sack of flour as I go. The white powder flies, temporarily blinding him. The man steps back, giving me enough time. I don't think about the contraption in my hand or what I'm going to do with it. I take my chance, my only chance. The tip of the man's gun drops enough that I have an opening and I take it. My arm swings down hard and fast, jabbing the meat thermometer into his face. I feel it sink into his eye.

Screaming, the man swipes at me with his weapon, making it clothesline me across my chest. The force sends me sailing backwards and I land on the floor. The man is shouting, clutching at his eye, and hurrying toward me. He raises his gun, ready to shoot. "You motherfucking—"

He doesn't finish his sentence. A loud crack fills my ears as I watch him fall to the floor with a bullet in his head. I'm standing before him with Amanda's gun grasped firmly between my hands, my elbows locked, and the gun still pointing to the place where he stood.

I don't remember picking it up. I don't remember anything.

Tremors rake through me, but I can't move from that spot. Rapid footfalls make me whirl around to the open front door. Sean is standing there, breathless. I can't move. I can't lower the gun.

Sean holds up his hands, "It's just me. Are you all right?" His voice is so wrong, so frightened. A swipe of dark red runs along his temple and drips onto his cheek. Sean looks past me at the dead man on the floor, before his wide blue gaze returns to my face.

Tears fill my eyes but don't fall. It feels like something is crushing me and I can't breathe. Gasping, I try to make sense of what happened, of what I've done. My grip on the weapon is so tight that I'm shaking, which makes it difficult to hold. Slick palms don't help either and as I squeeze the hilt hard, it slips from my hands and falls to the floor. My jaw drops and I don't know if I'm trying to gulp air or going to vomit. My knees give out as soon as the gun slips from my fingers and I crash onto the floor. The room tips sideways as it spins. Sean calls my name, but he sounds as if he's a million miles away. The edges of my vision flicker before everything fades to black.

CHAPTER 4

I wake to the sound of Sean's voice. It's low and urgent. "I don't give a fuck where he is. I'm flying into MacArthur Airport and I need him there. It's not optional." Sean's back is to me and he's breathing hard. I'm lying on the bed, covered in a mound of blankets. It's still night, so it surprises me when I glance toward the opening where the window had been and see a few men hoisting a new pane of glass into place.

"You're up." Sean is standing over the bed and looks down at me with such sorrow in his eyes that I can't hold his gaze.

I glance at the crew and back at Sean. "Yeah, I'm up." For a second, I tense and glance around, looking for the body, but it's gone.

Sean sits next to me and places a hand on my shoulder. The gentle touch makes me jump. "It's all right. Everything is all right. I made arrangements to get your arm looked at, but we need to get out of here."

I want to ask where the body went and a thousand other questions that are racing through my mind, but I just nod. Sean speaks to the crew again, and they assure him that the house will be restored to its original condition and that no one will know anything ever happened.

The crew leader is wearing dark jeans, a jacket, and a baseball cap. He's an older guy. He grins and says, "There won't be a single shard of glass anywhere when we're done."

Sean doesn't smile. He simply nods and looks the man in the eye. "Silence is worth its weight in gold. There are bonuses for those who finish early and keep things to themselves."

The guy smiles broadly. "Those are excellent terms, Mr. Ferro. I'm happy to do anything you need. Have a safe flight." The conversation ends and the crew works faster.

Sean takes my hand and we head toward the field. He's silent until we're in the hangar and boarding the plane. "Where's the pilot?" I glance around for him, but he's not here, and since Sean is climbing into the cockpit, I doubt he's coming.

Sean responds as he flips switches. "You saw him earlier tonight."

My throat tightens as the memories come rushing back. I'm standing, staring down at Sean. "Is he...?" Is he dead? He has to be, but I still have to ask. My stomach twists uneasily even though I already know the answer. I know what I've done.

"I'm sorry, Avery. I'm so goddamn sorry that you have no idea. That man worked for me forever."

I sit in the seat next to him as he does more stuff. The hangar doors part and the night sky fills my field of view. I was so excited on the way here, but now this place is filled with nightmares like the rest of my life. "I thought it was Henry." I blurt it out without thinking. It was just a gut feeling. Miss Black kicked his ass for messing with me and the guy has a key to my room. Add in the fact that I felt like someone has been in there and the mirror writing, and Henry is the only one that makes sense.

Sean doesn't respond. His dark brows are pinched together as we taxi down the short runway and lift into the air. He speaks into his headphones while I stare blankly out the window, watching the ground below grow further and further away. I had no idea he could fly a plane. I want to ask when he learned but part of me wonders if he actually has a license or if he's winging it. Sean doesn't seem like the kind of guy that would do things half way, but still.

"Henry Thomas hates me." Sean's face is stern and his voice gives no indication as to what happened between them. It feels like a button I shouldn't press, but some lunatic tried to kill me. This isn't the time to be shy.

"Why? What'd you ever do to him?"

Sean's jaw shifts from side to side. The tension across his face is the only reason I know he's upset. He's reverting to the robot version, hiding within himself. I don't think I can bear to watch that happen to him. I nearly laugh to myself, but swallow it. When we first met, I wanted to be like Sean— emotionally barren and immune to any feeling at all.

Now it sounds like Hell.

When Sean speaks, his voice is tense and low. "I took something from him that he wanted very much."

I'm watching the side of his face and the way his jaw tightens and shifts under the dark stubble lining his cheeks. Call it a gut feeling, but I think I know what Sean took. I look away and things start to snap into place. While glancing at the lights below, I say her name, knowing that I'm conjuring her ghost. "Amanda."

Sean doesn't respond. He doesn't have to. I know I'm right and that's the bad blood between them. Henry must have been in love with Amanda and then finding out that I was involved with Sean probably made him a little nuts. Okay, it made him very nuts. Damn.

Sean surprises me and speaks. "When I met Amanda she was with Henry Thomas.

He was about to put a ring on her finger, but I stole her away before he had the chance. Since then, he's pretty much hated me. But when she died, he lost it. I think he still loved her." Sean's voice fades until silence fills the air. The unsaid words are thick and press down on my chest, making it hard to breathe. Henry thinks Sean killed Amanda. He has no idea what really happened, which is gut wrenching. Sean's a good man, but no one sees it.

I'm biting my lip, thinking, feeling the sting on my arm, but sleep is pawing at me. Actually it's battering me with lion-sized bitchslaps. I feel so insane and sleepy, but there's a surge of energy still coursing through me. "Do you think Henry hired your pilot to kill me? Why would he want to kill me? I thought he liked me?" I flex my fingers and stare at my palms, not understanding. Something's not quite right, but I don't know what.

Sean glances at me. "I don't know. Maybe he's trying to inflict the same pain upon me that he suffered. Or maybe it has nothing to do with him." It seems like Sean is going to say something else, but his mouth snaps shut.

We fly on in silence. When he lands the plane, I'm ready to fall over. As we walk across the tarmac, the ground dips and sways beneath my feet. Sean's arm is around me and ushers me into a limo that's waiting for us. When I slip inside, I'm surprised to see someone.

Apparently, so is Sean because after he sits down and looks up, he angrily blurts out, "What the fuck are you doing here?"

CHAPTER 5

Bryan Ferro is slouched back against the opposite seat with one arm draped over the back. His dark hair obscures his green eyes. A brown leather jacket over a white shirt makes them look like gemstones in the darkness. There's a smirk on his lips, as if he knows how pissed off his presence will make Sean.

When I got into the car, I didn't see Bryan and nearly sat on him. When I try to move to the opposite seat, I can't. I'm too weak. I reach for the opposite bench—for the spot next to Sean—but my arm won't support me, so I fall forward.

Bryan jerks upright and reaches for me before I do a face plant into the other seat. "Whoa. What the hell happened?"

Sean leans forward and takes me from his cousin before pulling me into his arms. "None of your fucking business. Where's Logan? He said he'd be here."

Bryan's smirk is gone and doesn't return. His gaze shifts to the window. "Logan can't take her in through the hospital without everyone knowing. He sent me instead."

"And what the fuck are you supposed to do?" I lean into Sean's body and don't realize that I'm clutching my arm until I feel the sticky warm blood on my fingers. It's soaked through the bandage.

"I have connections." Bryan and Sean stare each other down, and a lifetime of unspoken words pass between them.

I'm too out of it to be polite. "Who's Logan?"

"My brother," Bryan replies. His tone softens when he speaks to me. His gaze shifts between Sean and me, finally settling on my face as if he's decided I'm the one to talk to. "Logan is working in the emergency room tonight. If you go in there, everyone will see you two. He's been practicing longer, but if it's just a few stitches, I know someone who will keep her mouth shut and fix you both up."

"I don't need anything," Sean snarls, "and I'm going to rip Logan's fucking head off the next time I see him."

Bryan smirks. "Yeah, we know. They talked about sending Joslyn so you'd be nice, but I volunteered because I knew you'd be a dumb fuck and not realize that you needed to be looked at too."

"Asshole."

Bryan's smirk doesn't fade. "Your head is bleeding, and as much as I love your company, I think your hooker friend could use some pain killers and a bed—assuming you won't tie her to it."

The muscles in Sean's arms feel like they're ready to pop. I understand what Bryan's saying. If I see Logan, what happened tonight can't remain hidden. The press will see us, and I know enough to realize what that will lead to—the dead body. I touch Sean's arm lightly and meet

Bryan's green gaze. "Take me to the other doctor. I don't want anyone to know."

Bryan nods and knocks on the window, indicating that the driver can go before slipping back into his seat and tucking his hands behind his head. He watches as I slump against Sean's side and hold onto my arm as tightly as I can. "Try not to do that. If you have glass in there, you'll make it worse."

I nod slightly. "Who's Joslyn?"

"His sister." Sean responds for him, his voice terse.

Bryan's eyes catch my ring and his grin broadens, but he says nothing. I wonder what his story is, and how he can be so perpetually happy. Every time I've seen the guy, he's had a smile on his face. It's like it was painted there and nearly nothing takes it away. "Twin sister, actually."

"Is that who we're going to see?" He'd said it was a woman, so I took a guess.

"Nah, someone else I know. She's doing her residency and we're actually crashing at her house. It's someone good, I promise. But we don't mention this to Jonathan—like ever. Okay? I had this number in case of apocalyptical disasters and shit like that. I'm pretty sure that this doesn't qualify, especially since it was given to Jon and I sort of took it."

Sean's eyes narrow. "What?" He's so annoyed that if he didn't have his arms wrapped around my shoulders, I'm pretty sure he would have strangled Bryan by now.

The ever-present grin lights up as Bryan's hands move, shooing us like it's no big deal. "Logan said Avery needed medical care and not to draw attention. This was the best way to do it. Why would you care if it pisses off Jon?"

Sean's jaw locks and I can tell he's biting back words. The world may think Sean is devoid of emotion, but I know otherwise. "Jon may not like me anymore, but I wouldn't intentionally betray his trust. Who is this person? What's the connection to Jonny?"

"The less you know, the better. You can blame the whole thing on me."

"No." Sean says firmly. "This is my mess, not yours. If Jon's pissed, it should be with me, not you."

Bryan laughs as he examines his nails. "How noble."

"It's reasonable." Sean's request is plain and rational, but Bryan doesn't cave in.

"Possibly, but I still can't tell you. You don't need to know and I don't need you taking hits for me. I can handle it, but thanks all the same." Bryan sits up and looks out the window. We crawl to a stop on a residential street. It's very early in the morning and the road is still shrouded in silence. "Wait here."

Bryan pushes the door open and slips out, closing it behind him, before dashing up the walkway to the front door. It's a grand house—not a mansion like the Ferro's—but much nicer than the home where I grew up. The house is two stories with a manicured front lawn, complete with sidewalks, on a picture perfect street.

Before Bryan can ring the bell, the door opens. A woman is standing there and looks past him to the car. She says something and retreats inside quickly, closing the door behind her. Bryan hurries back to the car and yanks the door open. "Come on."

Sean helps me up the walk and we follow Bryan around to a back door. My arm is causing me so much pain that there are tears in my eyes. I can't stop gritting my teeth even though I try. Every muscle in my body is corded tight, trying to deal with the agony.

When Sean ushers us inside, Bryan makes introductions. "Sean Ferro and Hooker Girl, meet Dr. Jennings."

CHAPTER 6

Why does Sean always take his bait? Before he can kill his cousin, I say, "Thank you so much for agreeing to look at me."

She nods, making her dark head of curls sway. Dr. Jennings isn't much older than I am. Actually, she looks too young to be a doctor. "Please, call me Mari. I'm not a doctor yet and don't thank me until we're done."

"You're not a doctor?" Sean asks bluntly.

Mari shakes her head, unfazed by his rudeness. "Not yet. Do you need a resume or do you want me to look you guys over?" Sean doesn't answer. Mari continues, "Okay then, let's see what you guys need. I don't even know if I'm able to help you here. Bryan called and said it was urgent." She holds out her hand and offers me a chair. Bryan and Sean stand behind me.

"Thank you. A window shattered and the glass cut my arm." As I'm talking, I offer Mari my arm. She unwraps the bloody bandages after pulling on plastic gloves. Her eyes sweep over the cut as she gently turns my wrist examining it closer.

"A window did this?"

I begin to explain, but Sean cuts her off. "Yes, and that's all you need to know."

Mari eyes him suspiciously and then smiles softly. She knows there's more story there, but it's almost like she doesn't believe the gash on my arm is from a pane of glass. "You need stitches, Mr. Ferro. Sit before you pass out."

Sean glances at Bryan, who seems like he wants to laugh. "Better do what she says. I'm not picking you up when you fall over. You're chunking up in your old age." Bryan gestures towards Sean's narrow waist with a flick of his hand before folding his arms over his chest.

"Prick."

"Dick."

"Wick," I add and giggle. All three of them look at me like I've lost my mind. "What? I thought we were rhyming." I laugh lightly and instantly regret it when pain shoots up my body and cracks my head in half.

I make a face and try to grab the wound, but Mari scolds me. "Don't. You two, out. Bryan, make sure he doesn't pass out. Go sit on the couch until I call you. Go on." When they don't move, she lifts a dark brow at them and adds sternly, "Now."

It surprises me, but they both vacate the kitchen, leaving us alone. Mari has a bag of stuff. She asks me a few medical questions before she gets to work on my arm, removing the bits of glass. It stings horribly, so she gives me a shot. "That should help, but it's going to make you feel sleepy. We can wait a few minutes. Most of the glass is out, but I want to make sure before we close it up."

The kitchen table is next to me. I'm leaning heavily on it with my good arm and pretty much staring at Mari. Her face seems familiar, but I'm certain I've never met her before. "So, how does Bryan know you?"

Her dark eyes dart away before she speaks. She tries to hide it, but her body tenses as if this isn't something she'd like to discuss. "A common acquaintance." It's not someone she wants to mention. I can tell from the way her eyes avoid mine and how she presses her lips into a thin line.

I don't know what her connection is to the Ferros, but I'm grateful for avoiding the hospital. "Well, thank you. I know it's weird, not wanting to go to the hospital." I glance up at her as she works silently.

After a few moments, she pauses and smiles softly. "It's all right. I understand." She tucks a curl behind her ear and looks up at me. "Are you sure there's nothing else you want to tell me?"

My eyebrows lift slightly. "Such as?" I glance around her kitchen. It's so pretty, with every surface gleaming like it's brand new.

"I don't know. It seems like a strange injury from a piece of broken glass. It looks like you were thrown through the window or something—as if someone did it on purpose. Avery, did he hurt you?" Her big brown eyes are filled with concern. She's a little thing, a waif of a person and it looks like she'd go kick Sean's ass right here and now if I said yes.

I smile. I can't help it. Everything about this woman is amazing. She took a stranger into her house in the middle of the night, and showed me more kindness than a friend would offer, and I don't even know her. Never mind that she overlooked the fact that I'm a hooker. She won major points for that. She didn't cringe when she patched me and has enough guts to ask if Sean is beating me.

"No," I say looking up at her, "he didn't do this. A stray bullet hit the window when I was standing by it. Sean covered me with his body as the thing splintered and came crashing down. He wouldn't hurt me."

Mari nods slowly. "Ah, that explains some things."

After the medicine starts to work, I can barely sit up. My mind goes foggy as she patches me and then helps Sean. We both have stitches that will dissolve, but Mari tells me to see a plastic surgeon because of the length of my wound.

Miss Black would have never hired me if I had a huge ass scar on my arm. I wonder if Gabe figured out that I stuffed my bracelet in the seat yet. He's going to be pissed. My mind swirls around that thought, over and over again. What is Black going to do when she finds me? The thought makes me shiver. I rub the goose bumps away and hear hushed tones passing between Mari and Sean.

He's standing, towering over her, trying to pay the woman, but she won't have it. Her slender arms fold across her chest. "No, I'm not taking your money. This was a favor." She turns her back on him and starts to pick up.

Bryan is sitting at the table with his head lowered, resting on his arms like he's asleep. He's said next to nothing all night. I have no idea who he is. In some ways he's like his cousin, Jonathan, all flash and charm, but there's something going on with him. He seems weary, like he's burdened by something he can't manage. He hides it with smiles the same way his cousin does.

"No," Sean says, following after her. "No favors. I have no idea who you are or what you'll do. We need to reach an agreement before I walk out that door."

Mari throws the rest of the bloody bandages in the trash and then snaps off her gloves and throws them in too. "You want an agreement? What, you think I'm going to blackmail you or something?"

"Or something." Sean is intimidating but Mari doesn't back down.

"Right, because the only reason to help someone is to take advantage of them later." She lets out a long annoyed sigh as she pinches the bridge of her nose. When she looks up, determination flashes in her tired eyes. "Listen, I did this because you know someone that I once cared about. That's it. If I saw you bleeding on the sidewalk, I would have done the same thing. I'm not going to bill you, blackmail you, or ever mention this again. If you want to pay me because your conscience can't handle kindness, then pay it forward. Show mercy and compassion to someone for no reason and ask for nothing in return. That'll make us square." Mari walks to the backdoor while she talks and leans on the knob. She twists it and tugs the door open, gesturing for us to go. "Now, if you don't mind, I need to be up and at the hospital in a couple of hours."

Sean's jaw locks tight. I know he wants to speak, but it seems like he doesn't know what to say. I'm pretty sure I'm drooling on myself, I'm so doped up on pain meds. My head feels like a sandbag, but I manage to stand and walk over to her. "I like you, Miss Mari. You're good people, and if I tried really hard, I don't think I could hope to be half the woman you are. You're like, a kick ass ninja of niceness." I'm clutching the front of her shirt and I think my words are coming out way too slow. She takes my hands so I don't rip her clothes off and tries to pull me upright.

Bryan appears next to me and laughs. "Easy there, Hooker Girl. I think you're going to make the woman blush if you keep going on and on like that."

"She's fine. It's just the medication." Mari says, but I can tell I made her uncomfortable.

While hanging onto Bryan, I add, "I would have said it anyway, probably more eloquently and without the ninja part if I weren't medicated." When I finish speaking, my pointer finger is pretty close to her face. I catch sight of my hand and wonder how it got there. Blinking hard, I drop it to my side.

Bryan turns me around and leads me out to the car, but I can hear Sean behind me, saying something that I don't understand. "You were too good for him."

"So people say," Mari replies softly, "and yet I imagine you've heard people say the same thing about her." Sean doesn't answer. "You're too quick to judge and too slow to forgive."

"How could you possibly know that?"

"Because I was the same way. Don't assume you know him—don't assume anything." She's speaking about a common acquaintance, but I have no idea who. Before I can hear more, my head is lowered and I'm seated in the car. Their voices turn to murmurs and I can no longer hear their words above the rustling of the trees and the engine.

When Sean climbs in a few moments later, I lean into his chest and fall into a deep sleep.

CHAPTER 7

The water is everywhere, dark and cold. Waves pelt into the sides of my face as I gasp for air, but get a mouthful of seawater instead. My limbs are frozen and I can no longer stay afloat. My neck sinks lower into the frozen ocean until my chin touches the waterline. I scream incoherently and manage to kick hard, forcing my neck up again.

Then the process repeats, over and over again, until my legs won't move. There's no air, only crushing waves, pressing on me, and pulling me under. My lips part to release a terrified scream that's been building within me, but there is no noise. Water floods my mouth, choking me, as panic laces its icy fingers around my neck and presses tight.

Terrified, I yell and dart upright. It's not dark and there's no water. My fists fly before I can figure out that I was dreaming. I suck in air and try to untangle myself from my bed as a hand lands on my shoulder. I react and my fists fly. Sean catches them and yanks me upright so I'm standing. "You're all right. You were dreaming, Avery."

He pulls me to his chest and holds me. As he strokes my head, I can see sunlight pouring into the room through the slats of the blinds. We're in my dorm room. My heart rate picks up again and I push away from him. My eyes dart around frantically. "Sean, this is a bad place to be. We shouldn't be here. Like, at all."

"Avery, trust me. I've thought about it and whoever is doing this has to be stopped. This is the safest place for you."

"But he has a key."

"Who?"

"Henry Thomas! At least I think it's him. Amber gave some guy a key and he snuck in here." I'm grabbing the sides of my head and tugging my hair. My muscles twitch as I force myself to stay still.

Sean nods and takes my hands in his. "Listen, I know you've had a hard night, but I need you to do what I ask you to do. We need to stop this. If it's Thomas, he'll show up. I have a feeling they won't wait long. This room is small and made of concrete. It's easier to protect you here and there are more people around. We just have to wait a few hours until night falls."

The corner of my mouth lifts. Sean talks like he's from another time. I lean against his chest and try to calm down. The dream is still with me, the feeling of ice on my neck remains even though it's over. I'm encouraged to take a shower and shake off the rest of my horrible dream. I let the steamy water beat over me, careful to avoid the stitches, but I can't stay in for too long. I need Sean. I need his arms around me and I have to hear him say that this will be all right.

After I pull on jeans and a tee shirt, I pad back to my bed and plop down next to Sean. He wraps his arms around me and kisses my forehead. "I'm sorry for this, for all of it."

I haven't wanted to think about the cabin, but now that we're away from it and I'm not in horrible pain, the images from the night before come rushing back. I feel like I'm going to be sick and press my hand to my lips as I mash them together. "I killed someone."

"You did what you had to do. He wasn't going to let you walk away. You had no choice, Avery. I just wish I'd gotten there sooner."

I understand what he means, that he would have killed the man. I don't know how I would have reacted to that either. Right now, I just want to throw up. Sean holds onto me loosely, stroking my messy hair, and wiping away tears as they silently stream down my cheek. When I'm able, I ask, "So, what now?"

"We lure the asshole here and take care of it."

I swallow hard and try to laugh about it. "I think I had this idea a while back and someone thought it was too juvenile to work."

Sean grins. "I reconsidered. It wasn't a bad plan."

It was a stupid and reckless plan, which is why we didn't do it last time. But what choice do we have? If this person can get at us through Sean's personnel, we're screwed. That means we can't trust anyone. For a moment last night, I wondered if Bryan was there to finish the job. God, I'm turning into a lunatic.

I pull away from Sean, sit on the edge of my bed, and bury my face in my hands. A torrent of emotions fills my chest and I have no idea which one to react to and which to ignore. That's been my vice—I'll wait and deal with it later. Well, it's later and this big fat mess bit me on the ass.

Clutching my hair in my hands, I stare at the floor and say, "What am I going to do? I fucked up school. There's no way in hell they're going to let me graduate, so I can kiss grad school goodbye too. Miss Black is going to be pissed and I doubt she's going to let me walk away, not after everything that's gone down. The other night at the hotel she tried to cover her ass and mine, and I screwed her over and disappeared. Gabe is going to take the brunt of my actions, and think I set him up at the hotel because I left my bracelet in his car without saying a damn word. Marty—I don't even want to think about how messed up stuff is with Marty. And Mel, damn—her life is fucking over, and it's all my fault. None of this crap would have happened if I didn't—"

"You can't think like that." Sean cuts me off, as he moves in front of me and looks down into my face. There is remorse in his eyes. He offers a weak smile. "Someone really smart told me that when my life turned to shit. She's tough, intelligent, and beautiful. And when the smoke finally clears, she'll pull through this the same way she pulled through everything else she's been through. We're survivors, Avery. We don't die. It's like we have an illness that makes us want to endure the worst."

I pick at the edge of my sheet, knowing exactly what he means. We had a conversation like this before, but last time it was about him. This time I feel the noose of guilt strangling me and I'd do anything to make it stop. I just want my life back and every moment of the past few days has gotten worse. My dreams are slipping through my fingers and now some lunatic is trying to shoot me.

I burst into tears in the most god-awful, snotty display imaginable. Sean's blue eyes widen in shock because my hysteria came out of nowhere. One moment I was totally serene, like I could logically process my thoughts and the next, Snotfest-a-palooza.

Sean sits down next to me, making the bed dip, and pulls me into his arms. I babble unintelligible sentences, trying to get out the fears and worries that are stabbing my heart. My entire body feels like it's going to die. My muscles tense and tighten until I'm ready to curl into a ball, but Sean won't let me. He doesn't release me, even though I tell him to. His shirt is covered in my sorrow and stained with my tears.

Sean takes my cheeks in between his palms and forces my gaze to meet his. "We'll get through this. There's no way in Hell I'm losing you now, so don't go cray cray on my ass. I don't know how to fix that."

His words catch me so off-guard that I blurt out a huge laugh, and wipe at my eyes. "You said cray cray."

"I'd say anything for you." Sean's voice is deep and determined. It feels like I was shoved over the edge of the abyss and have fallen into a never ending hole, but when he's with me, there's ground under my feet. The sensation of falling subsides and somehow everything seems like it might work out. I have no idea how, but maybe we'll be okay.

Sean leans in slowly with his intense gaze darting between my eyes and my lips. When he touches his mouth to mine a burst of tingles shoots through my body. Every inch is consumed with the light sensation and I instantly want more. Before the kiss has a chance to deepen, there's a knock at the door.

Sean pulls away and puts his finger to his lips and backs into Amber's closet, leaving the door cracked. He reaches for something in the back of his waistband before mouthing, "Open the door."

CHAPTER 8

My heart slams into my ribs, stealing my breath. Suddenly, I don't want to know who is on the other side. If it's someone I know, I don't think I could bear it, even if it's Henry. Maybe I'm stupid, I don't know, but I can't fathom the thought of being responsible for someone's death.

You already are, the voice in the back of my head says flatly.

What have I become? I don't want this to be my life. I want the picket fence and the little house. If I had a glittering pair of red shoes I'd be clicking the heels like mad right now, taking me and Sean out of this place. Why did Sean come back here? This was a horrible plan!

The knock comes from the door again and as I step toward it, time slows. I'm aware of the air around me, which is stagnant. The scent of stale smoke and Amber's perfume fills my head as I reach for the knob. I can't stand it. I want this to end, but I don't want it to be now. I've had enough. My brain is so fried that I can barely hold it together. Adrenalin races through my veins making me feel like I ate a crate of Pixie Stix. I can barely stand still. As I lift my fingers for the knob, they shake uncontrollably. Voices fade away so that the only sound I can hear is my heart.

My eyes sweep the room one last time. I glance at Sean peering through the door and take in the clock's glowing numbers blinking to 3:58pm. Amber's PJ's are on the floor like she rushed out this morning. Nothing is out of place, except for Sean hiding in my roommate's closet.

Dread trickles down my spine as I pull the door open. I try to throw a casual smile on my face, but I suspect it looks like I ate a live lobster and he's fighting to come back up. I'm staring at a guy that I've never seen before. He has tanned skin like he's outside often, with dark hair, and even darker eyes. He laughs and thrusts a clipboard at me. "Sign here and I'll bring it up."

"What?" I blink and remain where I am, standing on my side of the threshold.

"You have a delivery. I don't normally bring up packages this large to the dorms, but Central Holding didn't want it. They said to bring it directly to you." The man is still holding the clipboard, but I haven't taken it. "So I get to carry a hundred pound box up several flights of stairs." His dark brows pinch together before he removes his brown hat and cocks his head at me. "You did order a huge-ass package, right? A chair, couch, dresser—something like that?"

At the same time I say, "No," Sean appears behind me and says, "Yes."

The guy looks up at Sean and thrusts the clipboard at him. "Sign here." Sean takes it and signs, before handing it back. "I'll be back in a little bit."

Sean pulls me back into the room and closes the door. He runs his hands through his hair and looks at me sheepishly. I press my finger to his chest and ask, "What did you do, Sean Ferro?"

He grins—damn he's beautiful when he smiles like that—and runs his hands over the back of his neck, stepping away from me. "Nothing. An engagement present. It wasn't supposed to get here, yet."

"What is it?" Sean is acting so shy that my curiosity banishes every other worry floating through my head. What would make him act like that? What the hell did he get me? For a split second, I wonder if there's a woman in that box.

"I can't tell you. Wait and see—it's a surprise." He glances at the floor and then back up at me as bright patches of red stain his face.

My jaw drops. "Are you blushing?" I try to catch his gaze, but he won't look at me. I duck under his nose and chase him around the room for half a second before cornering him against the wall. "Mr. Jones, what could possibly make you blush?" Taking his chin, I make our eyes meet. "I'm a little nervous and very excited to find out the answer to that question."

"It's not what it is." He's smiling, laughing almost. He brushes my hand away and tries to push past me, but I don't let him.

"Then what is it?"

His lips curl as he tries to hide the smile that's on his mouth. He shakes his head and laughs. "You'll see soon enough."

"I hate waiting."

"I know." I stomp my foot and look out the window. "You are not going to help him carry it up here."

Folding my arms across my chest, I glance back at him. "Fine." How does he know what I'm thinking? I'm still not sure if I like that he can read my mind or if it freaks me out. I decide to turn things around on him, because I can read him just as well. Rounding on my heel, I march up to him, and poke his chest. "So, a little thought occurred to me."

Sean smiles down at me. "Really? And what's that?"

"When did you order this?" One of my brows lifts as the corners of my mouth twitch into a cocky grin. Sean's eyes dip to my cleavage, which is being thrust upward by my folded arms.

When he looks back into my eyes, he says, "When you weren't looking."

"You're always looking."

"Yes, I am. There's a lot to look at." Sean winks at me and my stomach dips. The man is sex on legs. Everything he does makes me melt.

I try to ignore the sensations flooding through me. "You're changing the subject, Mr. Jones."

"You're very perceptive, Miss Smith."

"So?"

He laughs and looks away, mirroring my pose. Sean's tight black T shirt hugs his arms and when he folds them, I can see each toned curve. The compulsion to drag my tongue across his muscles and then slowly lick his toned chest fills my mind. "Smitty?"

"What?" My imaginary lick was inching closer to his waist by the time I blink and glance up at him.

"You have that look on your face—the one that means your head is filled with dirty thoughts." He hooks his fingers in my waistband and tugs me toward him.

"My head is always filled with dirty thoughts when you're around. You broke me."

He kisses my cheek lightly. "I think you have that backwards. You were broken before and I fixed you." My smile fades as I look into his eyes. Sean cups my face and asks, "What is it?"

"This seems so impossible. I just want to be with you. Is that so hard?"

Sean lowers his head, inching closer for a kiss, when there's a bang at the door again. He releases me and gestures for me to open it. I wanted that kiss.

Crossing the room, I yank open the door and look up at the delivery guy. He's got a huge box—huge, as in I could live in it when I get dropped from all my classes next week—tied to a hand truck. I step aside and let him bring it in. Sean slips some money into the man's hand before he leaves. When the door closes, I race toward the box. There are no markings on it, no indication of what's inside.

"Are you sure this is safe? What if it's something bad?"

"It's not. I know what it is. You can open it."

I grin at him. It's one of those ear-to-ear smiles, and I pat the palms of my hands together as I decide which part of the super-thick box to pull apart first. What the heck is in there? I can't even imagine what would make him blush like that, after everything we've already done.

Sean pulls a knife from his waistband and slices through the tape. Well, it's good to know what he was reaching for before. He tucks the knife back behind him before saying, "Well, open it. I want to know what you think."

I squeal and yank at the cardboard, pulling back the sides of the box. The inside is reinforced and filled with a ton of packaging peanuts. I nearly fall into the container trying to swipe the little bits of foam away with my arm. Sean watches me silently with his arms across his chest and one hand by his lips. He's nervous. It's so cute, I could die.

I stop and look up at him with packaging peanuts clinging to my arms. "There is something in here, right? Or did you just send me an empty box? Because I'd be okay with that." I'm ready to dive in when Sean laughs and steps towards me.

He grabs my waist and yanks me back. "There's something in there. You can't jump in the box, you lunatic."

"I'm so playing with the box."

Sean laughs lightly and looks over his shoulder as he reaches into the box, digging around for whatever is in there. "Kids never want the toy, only the box. Maybe I should send this back?" When he stands, he has the corner of something. It's wrapped in opaque plastic, but it looks like the end of a couch.

Seriously? I stand there, staring, my jaw hanging open as he lifts out a backless sofa and puts it on the floor by the old one that's covered in Amber germs. The shape of the thing is really weird and not very tall. It looks like a bench that fell out of a Salvador Dalí painting.

Sean lets out a rush of air and turns to look at me. "Well?"

"You bought me furniture?"

"Not exactly. Open it." Sean steps away and slips his hands into his pockets. I can tell he's super proud of this present. I try to smile, like it's better than beans, but it's furniture. How's that romantic? Besides, there's a big empty box filled with packaging peanuts and it's totally calling my name.

I step toward the couchy thing and pull the wrapping off. When I'm done I'm looking down at a very modern piece of white furniture. It has sweeping, smooth lines that form two separate humps with a little place to sit in between. I start to smile, but try to repress my grin as I drag my fingers across the supple leather surface.

"Well?"

Oh fuck. He's so excited and I want to laugh my ass off. Why does this turn him on? Does he have a furniture fetish I'm unaware of? I have a goofy smirk on my lips when I sit in the center dip and look up at him. My mouth hangs open for a second, but the grin doesn't fade. I pat the curves of leather and finally manage, "Sean, I don't know what to say. I think you've seriously rendered me speechless."

His certainty fades. "Why?"

"Because, you bought me a camel-toe couch." I'm sitting there with an incredulous look on my face when Sean bursts out laughing. It's not the kind of light laugh when you think something is mildly entertaining, either. It's a full blown, belly laugh. I should have been a comedian. I'm a riot and seriously have no idea why he's laughing, because this is the ugliest couch I've ever seen. I'm not into modern. Even Marty knows that.

When Sean stops laughing he gives me a look. "You seriously don't know what this is?"

Obviously not, assuming his belly-laughter was any indication. So I pat it again and smile up at him, saying more certainly, "Of course I do. It's a one of a kind, camel-toe couch. For when yoga pants aren't enough. Do you have some weird thing for large horse-like animals with boobs that I need to know about, or does this stem back to a deranged camel-toe fetish?"

Sean doesn't reply. Instead the smirk slips off his face as he moves quickly. Before I know what happened, he's lifting me and then lowers me onto his lap. Sean sits under me in the center of the dip and my legs are wrapped around his waist. I gasp as he pushes me back against one of the leather humps and runs his hands up under my shirt, and cups my breasts. "It's a sex chair, one of the best in the world. Now I can have you anyway I want."

I'm still not getting it, so he shows me. He lifts and pivots me, before I sit back down on his lap, facing away from him. My feet reach the floor, making it easier to do things—like ride him hard and fast. He directs me to lean forward and lean against the larger curve of the couch. I do so and he kneels behind me, pressing against my backside. I can feel how much he wants me through his pants as he whispers into my ear, "Thinking of being with you on this chair has been driving me crazy."

My mind is filled with a lusty fog and my eyes are half closed. "I retract my previous statement. I like the chair better than the box."

"You never said you liked the box better."

"Oh?" I glance back at him and he pushes his hard length against my thigh, pressing me into the leather and stealing my breath.

"No." The corner of his lips twitch, as if he wants to smile. He tickles me until we're tangled together and I'm twisted back looking at his beautiful mouth, wanting things that we shouldn't do right now. "When does Amber get back?"

I shrug. "Sometimes she's gone for a few days at a time. She's kinda whorey and takes a bed wherever she can find one."

Sean doesn't wait for me to stop talking. His lips mash against mine as his hands slip under the hem of my shirt. In an instant, it's over my head and my bra is gone. Sean's warm hands run over my body, feeling my curves until he reaches my jeans. Breathing heavily, he nips my ear. "Turn away and stand up."

I do as he says and Sean strips me completely. I lean over the round part of the chair with Sean sitting behind me. I hear him moving and assume that he's getting rid of his clothing. Before I can look back I feel his hot mouth inching closer to my lower lips. He slips his tongue along my seam and I grip the chair harder, hugging it with my arms, as Sean teases me. Pressing his face between my legs, he licks deeper, and caresses my most sensitive parts.

Gasping for air, I dig my nails into the chair as his tongue goes to work, licking, sucking, and nipping me. Desire swirls through my body in hot waves as I try to hold back. I don't want to let go yet, but when he adds fingers I can't keep it together. My hips slam against his hand as he pushes inside of me, first one finger, and then two. I can't get enough of him.

"Come on baby."

"Not yet," I breathe.

"Oh? Do you like being teased?" I nod and his fingers disappear, followed by his hot mouth.

"No!" I feel frantic and am ready to turn around when I feel his fingers wrap around my inner-thighs and push my legs further apart. He presses his naked body against mine, sliding his length against me. I moan and try to shift so he slips inside of me, but Sean holds my hips in place.

"We're teasing you right now, Miss Smith. Be still."

I don't listen and try to shift and make him press into me. I'm rewarded, uh, I mean punished, with a slap to my backside. My right cheek stings and I stop moving. "Good girl."

Sean drags his hardness against me, shifting his hips and pushing, but never slipping inside. One of his hands presses my back down while the other reaches around to the V in my legs. His fingers stroke the slick folds at the very front. I can barely tolerate it. My body tries to writhe, but Sean holds me down, pressing his elbow into my back. I clutch the sides of the chair harder and beg him for things I'll never admit. I want him so badly that the teasing has turned to torture. I'm begging for him anyway he'll take me, and feel no shame.

That's when he moves me. I don't ask what he's doing for once. I just follow, still pleading with him to fill me with come. "Please, baby." I say the words over and over again as he directs me to lay back and lean my head off the top of the chair.

Before I can ask what he wants, his dick is against my cheek. I take him in my mouth and wrap my tongue around his hard, hot shaft, licking and sucking as I do so. Sean's body stiffens as he moans. I reach for his hips and encourage him to push in farther and he does. His length fills my mouth all the way to the back of my throat. I want to take all of him. I want him to ride my face and cry out my name as he fills my mouth with his sweet taste.

My nails claw into his ass as I rock his hips. Sean pushes in and pulls out, slowly at first. I suck him and push his hips harder toward me every time he pulls away. When he pushes all the way in, I suck in at the same time, and his length slips deep into my mouth and down my throat. Sean sighs and holds my head in place for a moment before pulling out. Then he does it again. Each thrust makes me wetter. I want to taste him and feel that hot, slick come pour down my throat. Sean presses deeper and faster, moaning as he does it. I think he's going to lose it, but then he pulls away.

Sean's gasping for air as he yanks my wrist and positions me without words. I stand against the back of the chair and lay down against the leather, facing away from him. Sean always has me facing away from him. One day, I hope he'll want to see me while he rides me. For now, this is enough, and it's sexy as hell to feel like this. He controls me, commands me, and I like it that way.

Sean spreads my legs after leaning me over the edge of the chair. He rubs himself against my hypersensitive, slick skin before sinking deep within my silken core. At first he holds my neck down and rides me from behind, pushing long and deep. Each thrust shoots tingles through my body, and builds my need for him. I beg him for more and his hand leaves my neck and finds a wrist. Then his other hand does the same and he pulls my arms back behind me, lifting me from the chair so that my breasts hang in the air. I moan as he does it, feeling him touch me from within, rousing sensations that I've never felt before. Sean remains still for a moment and then starts to rock. His hips push harder and faster.

I cry out, begging him for more. "Please, Sean. Please."

Until this point, he's been holding back, controlling himself, and it's totally obvious the moment he lets go. His body slams into mine with more force, pushing his shaft deeper and deeper within me. His hands clutch my wrists like iron, yanking me backward toward him with each thrust. My breasts bounce as my hair flies. I glance up and notice Sean watching me in the mirror. Our gazes lock as his speed increases. Neither of us looks away.

I don't think about what I look like or anything but how much I want him to come inside of me. I want that hot liquid to fill me and release me from my torment. As if he can read my thoughts I see the tension increase on his face. He pushes harder and faster, shoving deeper, until I lose it. My body reacts to his and there's nothing gentle about it. I scream his name, coming hard, and feel the rush of my excitement dripping between us.

Sean growls, clutching my wrists harder, and slows his thrusts as he loses himself. I watch his face in the mirror as his eyes clench closed and he uses my body to sate his need. When I feel Sean's cock pulsing, his eyes open and he watches me. Slowly, he pushes in and holds himself deep within me.

We stay like that for a moment and it's perfect, with both our bodies covered in sweat and locked together. I don't want to move. I don't want it to be over. Sean seems to read my mind, and we stay like that, watching each other in the mirror. When my arms begin to tremble and ache, Sean releases me and pulls out. I lay face-down on the chair and run the pad of my finger along a seam.

A moment later, Sean is there, crouching in front of me. "Miss Smith."

"Mr. Jones." I smile with a lazy sated grin.

He leans in with a devilish look on his lips that makes butterflies erupt in my stomach. "Now that we've tried out the chair, I think it's time to sample the box." He stands and holds out his hand.

I giggle and sit up, not quite understanding him. Taking his hand, I ask, "Sample?"

"Yes, sample." He takes my hands, sweeps me up in his arms, and twirls around. I shriek and cling to his slick, naked body, before he stops over the box. "First we need to fill it with something."

"Do you mean me or the box, because I think you already filled me rather well."

Sean kisses my nose and drops me. I fall the short distance into the packaging peanuts and yelp. When I look up at Sean, I stick my tongue out at him. "Very mature." He finds his phone and asks, "May I?"

My heart skips a beat. I have no idea what he wants to do, but I say, "Yes."

CHAPTER 9

A boyish smile crosses Sean's lips as he takes a picture. "One to remind me that the box can be as much fun as the present." The corner of his mouth tips up and he laughs, before pushing his dark hair out of his eyes. It's damp and laying in thick waves, almost as if it wanted to curl.

The moment is surreal. I'm lying in a box, surrounded by those earth-friendly packaging peanuts, half covered. My breasts are bare and my hair is over one shoulder.

My body is still slick with sweat and the little pieces of foam are sticking to me.

As I lay there, breathing slowly, I twist a lock of hair and look up at him from under my lashes. My mind wanders into the future, of what it will be like to become this man's wife. He bought me a sex chair for an engagement gift, and then this. I've never laid in a box naked before, and certainly not with someone watching, and that's what Sean does—watch. His eyes sweep over my bare curves, drinking in each one, savoring the glimpse as if he might not get another.

Every time I breathe my lungs fill and my chest lifts. His gaze drifts back to my breasts and lingers. His lips part like he wants to say something, but he doesn't. The phone remains in his hand, but he doesn't take more pictures or record anything. Instead, he stares until he finally says, "Avery, there's something I want to tell you."

I feel so sated and serene. My mind is lost in Lustland and all serious thoughts are scattered. I extend my hand toward him, inviting him to join me. Sean steps forward and takes my hand, but that's it. "Avery," he tries again and I can tell that the conversation is going to wipe that look off his face, so I stop him. I want him to be happy and it's so damn rare.

I won't let the moment go. I can't. "Close the lid." I know those three words will stop him. It's a total derailment and I can see the mental train wreck on his face when I offer.

"What did you say?" his voice is a breath, barely audible.

"Close me in." I take a deep gulp of air and bite my lips. The claustrophobic girl is asking to be locked in a box. I'll be terrified, just the way he likes it. The offer is too great to pass up.

"You're diabolical." He doesn't blink and I can tell he's torn. Part of him does not want to do it to me, but the side of Sean Ferro that loves to dominate and instill fear is prowling, ready to pounce. I see that dark hunger in his eyes, the need that's been evading him for too long.

"You know you want to do it. I won't offer again. Close the box." My lips part, and I breathe harder as my heart picks up the pace. If he closes me in, I'll totally freak out. The corners of my lips twitch as if they wanted to smile.

Sean watches the movement, but says nothing. He stands over me and takes one side of the box top and lifts it up before lowering it into place. My heart lurches inside as my hands tense at my sides. Our eyes are locked. It's almost like I'm daring him to do it and I have no idea how long he'll leave me in here. Even so, I don't look away. My chin lifts slightly as I fill my lungs. Sean reaches across me and grabs the other flap. He lowers it slowly, increasing the effect of the shadows closing in around me. My pulse picks up as my eyes dart around the box. Suddenly, I want to jump up and stop him, but I don't. I force myself to remain still, my eyes are glued to his.

Sean leans in close. When he speaks, his voice is so deep. "Last chance to bow out, Smitty."

I love it when he calls me that. I shake my head. "I'm as twisted as you are, remember?"

"I know, and I love it." His eyes are hungry, and I know how much he wants this—how much he needs it. I wonder why he hasn't asked. I would have let him. Before I can say another word, Sean closes the lid.

~ 72 ~

CHAPTER 10

I'm fine. I tell myself even though I'm already beyond nervous. There is a tiny shaft of light that slices through the darkness, so I know that there's air in here, even though it doesn't feel like it. I try to close my eyes and forget where I am, but I can't. The foam peanuts remind me that I'm inside a tiny space with very little air. There's no breeze across my skin, nothing.

My hands have found the sides of the box and just before I push on the lid, I hear a noise—tape. The seam of light across the top of the box disappears. I gasp and try to sit up as my palms splay against the top of the box. He wasn't supposed to trap me in here.

Yes, he was. You knew he wouldn't let you out. It's part of the game.

Even so, I can't stand it. I try to calm myself and lay back in the foam. I count my fingers and toes until each one is so tense that I can't tolerate it. I feel my mind unraveling. When I open my eyes it looks the same as when they're closed. I can't see anything. There's not enough air. That's when the panic rises up my throat and starts to wrap its fingers around my throat. I reach out and claw at the sides of the box and start kicking and thrashing. I call for Sean to let me out, but he doesn't answer. The tape doesn't rip away and the lid doesn't open.

My chest constricts as my heart pounds harder, faster. Pressing my palms above my head, I push hard. When that doesn't work, I try my legs. What the hell did he use to seal the box? The lid won't budge. I call his name again and bang on the crate, but no one comes.

Gasping, I try to silence my fears, but I can't. They control me, they choose my words, and the pitch of my voice. They make me say things and beg. I claw at the walls and throw the foam, but that only makes it worse. As the packaging peanuts slip over me, their jagged edges feel like bugs and my mind flashes an image of a casket. That dream, the one where I'm buried alive, ignites behind my eyes as terror shoots through my veins.

I have no idea how long I've been in here, but I can't separate rational thought from nightmares. I scream and feel beetle legs pricking my skin. They're stuck in my hair and trying to devour me. The darkness drips with menace and a horrified scream rips from my mouth. My nails scratch at the cardboard as tears streak from my eyes.

The lid suddenly opens and I'm blinded by light. Before I have time to move, a body is on top of mine, naked and aroused. The lid closes behind him and the darkness covers me. Before I can scream, his hand covers my mouth. At the same time, he moves and slams his hard body against mine, forcing himself between my legs and inside of me.

I hear Sean's voice in my ear, but it sounds like he's a million miles away. As his hips pound against me over and over again, he makes guttural sounds every bit as monsterish as he thinks he is. My entire body is tense, not welcoming, but that doesn't stop him. Sean crushes into me, pushing deeper and harder with each thrust. His hand over my mouth makes me feel like I'm being suffocated, but the other hand, the one on my hips is gentle. Sean's fingers glide along my skin, tracing the curve. The action stands in stark contrast to the rest of his behavior, but I can't think. There's nothing but blackness and death and I'm trapped, lost in a scream that never ends.

When Sean's thrusts slow my eyes shoot open. I didn't realize I'd been pinching them shut. I can make out the side of his cheek in the darkness. The sliver of light allows me to see just a little bit. Sean's lips are parted and his eyes are shut. He's lost, and I wonder if he knows he's fucking me at that moment or if it even matters.

When he finally pushes into me one last time, it feels like I've been rubbed raw. He shudders as he fills me, and the stinging abates when he pulls out. Sean releases his hold on my mouth and pushes the box open. Without a word he stands and steps out. He doesn't look down at me, ask me if I'm all right, or offer his hand.

I lay there with the lid open and shiver, half seeing my dorm room ceiling and half blinking away images of the funeral home. I stared at the ceiling for hours when my parents died. I know every inch of that funeral home and one day it'll be me laying there.

"Breathe." The command breaks my thoughts and my eyes cut to the side. Sean is standing there naked, and staring down, like he can't stand the sight of me.

I should hold my breath to spite him. *What happened?* A small logical voice in the far corner of my mind sounds out, asking the obvious question. *Why is he angry?*

I don't know.

I suck in air and Sean turns his back on me again. "Do you have towels?"

"They're in the bathroom. Through that door." I jab my thumb in the right direction and Sean disappears into the tiny room. I hear the water turn on. He doesn't invite me in.

I lay in the box, staring at the ceiling, wondering if I should ask him the questions floating through my mind. I don't feel like moving. Actually, I want to cry. Why did I let him do this to me? I liked it at first, but not this time. What was different? I don't understand, but I need to know.

CHAPTER 11

I push up and brush off the foam, before padding into the bathroom. The little room is filled with steam. Sean is standing silently in the shower with his head down and the water beating over his neck. I can see his outline when I walk in. He doesn't move or look over at me.

I make sure the doors are locked and pull open the curtain. He won't meet my gaze. "Sean?"

"I shouldn't have done that." His voice is level, even. There's no hint of remorse even though his words were an apology. He's shutting down, and locking me out. I won't know what's going on inside his head if I don't jump in now. It might already be too late.

I don't know what to say so I start talking. "You don't have to fix everything by yourself. We made a mistake."

This makes him glance up at me. The water runs down his cheeks and shoulders. There's no expression on his face. I can't read him at all. There's no clue to what he's thinking other than his words. "It was my error, not yours."

I step into the shower with him. "Maybe it wasn't a mistake. Maybe it was something else. I liked it last time—the time in the elevator. The feelings were similar, but this time they derailed. I don't understand why."

Sean closes his eyes and turns away from me. He rinses off and tries to step out, but I grab his wrist. I flash my ring at him. "I'm going to be your wife, remember? We take chances together and when they don't work out, we fix them. This didn't work. I need to know why."

Sean doesn't look at the ring. He just stares at me with that arrogant look in his eye, like he knows but won't tell me. "No, you really don't. We won't do it again, so put it out of your mind."

He tries to pull away, but I don't let him. "Sean!"

"Avery, not now. Don't push this. Leave it alone." The steadiness in his voice is gone. There's a slight tremor, a warning note to let me know not to push him, but I have to. I can't let it go.

"Just tell me."

"You don't need to know."

"Like Hell I don't! Do you even know what I just gave you? You owe it to me! Tell me what I did wrong!" I'm yelling in his face, ready to cry.

Sean's shoulders square and I know I won't get an answer from him. I turn on my heel quickly and drag the curtain closed, before pressing my forehead to the wall. The tile is cold against my skin and the water disguises my tears. I don't sob, but I can't stop the rest. It feels wrong.

A moment later the curtain opens. Sean's voice is soft. "It wasn't you, Avery. You didn't do anything wrong. I'm—I fucked up." I turn slowly, but avoid his eyes. My arms are wrapped around my middle as the water pounds over me. Sean continues, "Sometimes I can't sort between the past and the present. I don't want to hurt you, and the truth will hurt you more. I don't want to say the rest. I mean, I don't think I should."

I lift my chin and meet his somber gaze. Shaking my head, I press him, urging, "Let me in."

"Not this time, Avery."

"You were somewhere else. I was someone else. If you say it, if you admit it, it'll stop. Purge your soul, Sean. Just do it. Whatever I'm going to imagine is going to be worse than what you were thinking anyway."

Sean just shakes his head and turns from me with his jaw locked tight. Whatever past he was reliving, it terrified him as much as it terrified me.

CHAPTER 12

The rest of the afternoon passes slowly. I try not to think about what happened, but the box is still in the room and it reminds me. I close the lid and shove it to Amber's side of the room before laying on my bed. We're waiting for death to come knocking. I wonder how mental I am that I don't care. My life is so out of control, so completely messed up, that I welcome the knock. I won't jump off a ledge or anything, but I hurt so much… I just want it to stop.

Sean doesn't say much. He's upset with himself, of that I'm certain. He's on my computer, doing God knows what, when he finally asks me, "Were there more videos from the sexting client that weren't deleted?"

My eyes cut across the room to the little desk, and I sit upright on my bed. "Yes. Why?"

Sean's lips are pressed together. "Come see."

"I don't care." I stay on my bed and lay back down. So what if another video of me is out there? That's the least of my problems at the moment.

"I need to know if it's a copy or if this was from a different time." Sean's voice is tense.

I push up and walk over to him before glancing past his shoulder at the screen. Sean presses play and I don't know what I'm looking at. It's very dark, too dark to make out faces, but I know it's me. The floor of my stomach drops. "I didn't record that." As the video continues, I see me having sex with someone, but there's no face—just a naked back. He's in my room, on my bed, slamming his hips into mine. My hands fly to my mouth as I try not to scream because I don't remember doing that at all. "Who is that? Where'd you find this?"

"It's online on some no name website with a low ranking. It doesn't seem like he's used it yet. Are you sure you didn't do this? I mean, I know you had other clients. You don't have to spare me, Avery."

I smack the back of his head. Sean winces and turns quickly before I can do it again. "No! I'm not a goddamn slut! I know who I slept with and I don't know who that is. I haven't had sex with anyone in this room, besides you."

"I had to ask. I didn't mean to upset you." Sean makes a copy of the video and hits replay, watching the damn thing over and over again on mute.

I finally ask, "What are you doing?"

He doesn't say anything for a while. When he turns around he says, "This is me. Someone edited it and put in a different guy."

"How can you tell?" I look at the video over his shoulder.

"There are a few spots where he didn't take out my hand. See?" Sean stops on a frame and I can make out his ring on his finger between the bed sheets. "Fast forward a frame or two and it's gone."

"How'd you even find this?" I'm staring at the screen wondering who would make a fake sex video of me, but that's the question I ask.

"The IP address matched an email I received a while back. The letter was nice enough, but it just seemed off. I've been digging around looking for more to pop up, but nothing did—until now."

"Do you think it's Henry?" I ask nervously.

Sean shakes his head. "Does it look like Henry?"

"It wouldn't have to be him in the video."

"No, Henry Thomas had a crush on you. If he made this, he would have used his own image and made things more visible. He would have emailed it to me to show off his trophy. This isn't like him." Sean stares at the screen for a while longer, silent.

I go back to my bed and lay down. My phone chirps. There's a message from a number I don't recognize, but I know it's from Mel.

B SAFE. U OWE ME A STACK WHEN THIS SHIT IS DONE.

I text back.

K. IHOP IT IS.

I want to ask her where she is and if she's all right, but I know better. This is safer. Some lunatic is trying to kill me. If they're trying to clean up their mess, they'll be after Mel too.

Sean doesn't ask who I'm texting. Instead, he comes and sits next to me on the bed. He changes the conversation. "No sex for a while, okay?" His voice is too serious to be joking.

I don't like it. I want my Sean back, the one that's all smiles. "Okay, but what am I supposed to do with my camel-toe couch?"

He grins and bumps his shoulder into mine. "I need to work some things out, so what happened today doesn't reoccur. Give me a little time, if you can." Sean has his hands clasped in front of him and is looking down. His dark hair obscures his eyes and the slant of his shoulders lets me know how upset he really is.

"Sean, I love you. I'd give you anything and everything." I put my arm around him, but he flinches. My smile fades as I take my hand back and slip it into my lap. "No touching? Sean, talk to me. Please." *I can help you.* Those are the words I so desperately want to say, but I wonder if I can. What if I can't and I just make it worse. Whatever happened today, whatever past he slipped into is a reality that he wants to erase. But the past can't be wiped clean. There are no do-overs and the chalk outline will always be there no matter how many times we try to wipe it away.

"One day, Avery, just not today." He won't lift his face. I think I finally understand what he means, although it isn't what he says.

Whatever he did, whatever happened in the past, he can't admit it to himself yet—so he can't tell me. Not yet. "Okay, but I'm going to have trouble with the no touching thing."

"That won't last long. It's the aftershocks." He finally turns his head and looks into my eyes. "You're amazing. I don't deserve you. I know I don't."

I offer a lopsided smile and resist the urge to throw my arms around him. It'd be like setting off a bomb and he's already covered in shrapnel. Why do good intentions turn to crap?

Stop it. Stop feeling sorry for yourself. There she is, that voice within me—the part of me that's sick of complaining and excuses— she's the savage part of me, comprised of a drop of animal instinct combined with raw rage that's kept me alive this long. *Everyone steps in shit. They keep walking and it comes off. Move, Avery. Let Sean deal with his crap and you deal with yours.*

My spine straightens and my voice is more certain when I speak. "We deserve each other. There's no one I'd rather be with—ever. Get used to the idea, because I'm not changing my mind."

CHAPTER 13

We pull out Monopoly, the world's longest game, and eat Amber's bitch stash. It's mostly chocolate and carbs. I'm starving, but Sean doesn't want to order pizza or leave the room. No one saw him sneak in and he's hoping the delivery didn't mess up his plan.

As I stuff a Hershey bar into my mouth, I glance at Amber's bed. "Where the hell is she?" Normally I'm glad when the roommate from hell is gone for this long, but she usually stops in and whines, before going back out. I haven't seen her yet.

Sean moves his little silver shoe and goes straight to jail. His dark eyes lift to meet mine. "That feels like an omen."

"Maybe we should pull out her Ouija board." I glance at Amber's bed again.

"I thought you said she didn't come back every night."

"She doesn't, but it's day time. Trolls have to hide during the day. It's a state law." I move my thimble and draw a card. "Fork over $50. I won a beauty pageant." I strike a pose and giggle.

Sean tosses me the paper money. "This would be more fun with real currency. Who the hell wins $50 at a beauty pageant anyway? That's like winning 50 cents."

"Nah, you'd be out at least $450 on a dress. Unless it's a birthday suit contest. I don't think the Monopoly man hosts those kind of events."

Sean sniggers and rolls. No doubles, so I go again while his shoe hangs out in the slammer. "So, what's the plan?"

Sean's eyes dart away from mine as he leans back on his elbow. "There is no plan."

"Yeah, I'm sure." I move a few spaces and pay $2 in rent.

Sean takes the money from me. "Wow, thanks for this. I'm rich."

"Snob," I tease.

"Am I so out of touch with reality? Very well, Miss Smith, where can I find boarding for $2?"

"There's a lovely box that I'm subletting." I hold out my arms like a game show hostess toward the corner of the box by Amber's bed.

He tosses a little plastic house at me. I make a face and start to peg him with hotels. "That wasn't nice, Mr. Jones!" As I say it, I take the bank tray, stand, and dump it on his head. All the fake money flutters around him. A $500 bill sticks to his shirt and another is in his hair.

Sean grins. "Now I feel better."

I chuckle and wish that I could pounce on him and tickle him until he cries, but I keep my seat. I'll have to wait until he's ready to touch me again. I hate waiting. "Oh, good. Then here, have some real estate too." I lean forward and start tucking cards in his shirt and then put another behind his ear and then another in his pocket.

Sean grabs my wrist before I manage to touch him. He immediately realizes that I wasn't going to touch him and drops my hand. "Sorry."

I shrug. "Don't be." After a moment of silence, I add, "I won't hurt you, Sean."

He sits up and pinches the bridge of his nose, like he has a massive headache. "Avery I need to tell you something."

Before he can say more, there's a knock at the door. Our eyes meet and hold for a second before Sean jumps up and slips into Amber's closet, again. It's next to the door and slightly behind it. A second knock doesn't come. Instead, the metallic sound of a key slips into the lock.

I remain on the floor, like I was throwing fake money over my head. This is it—this is the madman that's been shooting at me, the person who hired the pilot to kill me. This deranged nutjob wants me dead and I have no idea why. My skin covers in gooseflesh as the knob turns. I don't move, I don't hide. This is it. One of us is leaving this room in a body bag and it won't be me.

Nausea washes over me as the door is pushed open.

Breathe, Avery. Just breathe.

When the door moves my heart shudders and stops. A slender woman, dressed in black, is flanked by two men. Her face is devoid of emotion, but her eyes are lethal and shooting daggers at me.

I stammer, "Miss Black."

She steps into the room with the men. "Close the door," she directs in that chillingly cold voice of hers. "I have things to discuss with Avery. Gabe, check the room. You, stay by the door." Miss Black snaps her fingers and both men do as she asks.

I wonder if Gabe will say anything when he finds Sean. He checks the entire room and for a moment, no one breathes. He looks in Amber's closet and moves on, not making any indication that Sean is inside.

Miss Black snaps her fingers at me. "Sit." She points to my bed before folding her arms across her chest and tapping her foot.

I don't know what Sean is doing, so I move slowly, asking questions. "When did you get a key?"

She smirks. "Dear Avery, I've had a key this entire time. Do you really think I wouldn't? What if you didn't show up one morning? What if you suddenly disappeared off the face of the earth? How else would I find out if you were dead in your room?" Her voice drops an octave when she says the last sentence.

I sit stiffly on the edge of my mattress and try not to look at Gabe or the place where Sean is hiding. "Are you threatening me?"

She laughs. The woman actually presses her tapered fingers to her red lips and chortles. "I'm capable of so many things. It's nice to see you on your toes, isn't it Mr. Ferro?" My eyes remain locked on Black. I'm afraid that I've looked at the closet too many times, but I haven't. A moment later, Sean steps out, knife in hand. It's the kind hunters use to gut things. It has a sharp blade and a thick hilt. "Charming, but not necessary."

"I'll decide what's necessary," Sean replies.

She smiles, but it's the grin of a carnivore prior to devouring its prey. She steps towards Sean in her fuck-me high heels. Miss Black stops in front of Sean and presses her finger to the tip of the blade, nicking her skin. A bead of scarlet forms on her fingertip. Her dark eyes watch it for a second before saying, "Your preferences are peculiar Mr. Ferro, even for me." She takes a white handkerchief from her coat pocket and dabs her finger before continuing. "But for the girl who will do anything with anyone, well..." She ends the thought with a wink and turns toward me.

Sean is tense, standing before her with his jaw locked tight. "I wonder if Miss Stanz knows the complexities of your desires."

I don't like this. Something feels way the butt off. "Just shoot me if that's what you came for."

Miss Black arches a perfectly plucked eyebrow at me like I'm an idiot. "Who bites the hand that feeds them? I mean, really, Avery. You should be ashamed of yourself. I gave you your life back and offered you so much more and this is how you repay me?" She reaches for my hand and looks at my engagement ring, before rolling her eyes. "How many of these have you handed out now, Mr. Ferro. Tell me, do you get a baker's dozen discount from the jeweler?"

I glance between Sean and Black, catching her meaning right away. I expect

Sean to deny it, but he's silently clutching the gleaming blade in his hand. I don't know if he's frozen with fear or if he's plotting his next move. Either way, I don't like it.

"More fiancées?" I murmur.

"Yes, of course. You didn't think you were his one and only. I mean, why would you when there's information right at your fingertips? Oh, that's right. You have this juvenile notion of trust. Well, here, Avery dear, let me spell it out for you." Miss Black steps next to me and laces her arm over my shoulder and points at Sean with her other hand. "Mr. Ferro currently has two fiancées—you and the woman in California. That one got the better deal if you ask me. She's in that posh mansion while you're stuck in this hell hole." She glances around my dorm room and sneers.

I shake her off and step toward Sean, not believing a word of it. "She's lying, right? Tell me it isn't true." But as I stand there and look into his eyes, I can see that it is. "Sean." I gasp his name as if it were a stake through my heart. I can't breathe. Sean doesn't deny the accusation, nor does he explain himself. "Say something. How could you?"

I want to walk over and pound my fists into his chest. Has he really been playing me this whole time? Sean ignores my questions and directs his statement at Black. "Your man is dead."

Black's smile turns to a sneer. "I suppose you'd do something like that." Sean doesn't answer. "Quite reactionary." She shakes her head as she examines her nails. When she glances up at Sean, she adds, "Miss Stanz is leaving with me. Pay the rest of your balance in the morning. Thank you for babysitting her while I sorted things out."

"Sean?" I gulp air, trying to breathe. "What is she saying?"

"Just go with them. Walk out the door and don't look back. You'll be fine." Sean says it like I should trust him, like I should just go, but I can't. Gabe places a hand on my arm and starts to pull me toward the door, but I slip out of his grip.

"No! Someone tell me what the fuck is going on!"

Miss Black pinches the bridge of her nose and sighs. "Everything always has to be the hard way with you. Fine. So be it." Black snaps her fingers and before I know what happened, I'm shoved backward. I expect to fall and hit the floor, but I land in the box. Packaging peanuts go flying as the wind is knocked out of me. Before I can react, someone stabs me with a syringe. The room spins and tips as I try to keep my eyes open, but I can't.

My eyes lock on Sean's as the lid is closed and the shadows swallow me whole.

COMING SOON

BROKEN PROMISES

A Trystan Scott Novel

Read more about the characters
in this book:

BRYAN FERRO
~THE PROPOSITION~

*****

SEAN FERRO
~THE ARRANGEMENT~

******

PETER FERRO GRANZ
~DAMAGED~

******

JONATHAN FERRO
~STRIPPED~

******

TRYSTAN SCOTT
~COLLIDE~

MORE ROMANCE BOOKS BY

H.M. WARD

DAMAGED

THE ARRANGEMENT

STRIPPED

SCANDALOUS

SCANDALOUS 2

SECRETS

THE SECRET LIFE OF TRYSTAN
SCOTT

And more.

To see a full book list, please visit:
www.SexyAwesomeBooks.com/books.htm